DO DONUTS FALL IN WINTER?

Library of Congress Cataloging-in-Publication Data

Woodworth, Viki.
Do donuts fall in the winter? / Viki Woodworth.
p. cm
Summary: Simple, humorous rhymes ask a series of questions
about things that appear in the winter.
ISBN 1-56766-222-6 (hard cover : lib. bd.)
[1. Summer—Fiction. 2. Stories in rhyme.]
1. Title.
PZ8.3.W893Dod 1996   95-44668
[E]—dc20   CIP / AC

DO DONUTS FALL
IN WINTER?

by Viki Woodworth

Viki Woodworth and family.

When winter arrives,
what falls from
the sky?

A dog?
A donut?
Snow
or a tie?

(Snow)

What has no leaves
in the cold
winter time?

A tiger?
A tree?

A candle
or dime?

(A tree)

Who eats the food
that it stored
in the fall?

A dancer?
A dress?

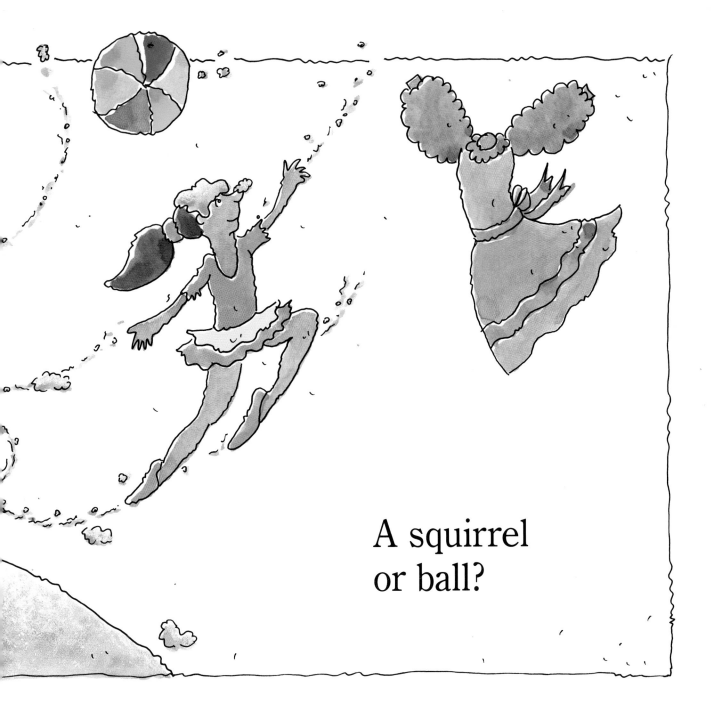

A squirrel
or ball?

(A squirrel)

Who sleeps through
the cold,
wind and ice?

A bottle?
A bear?

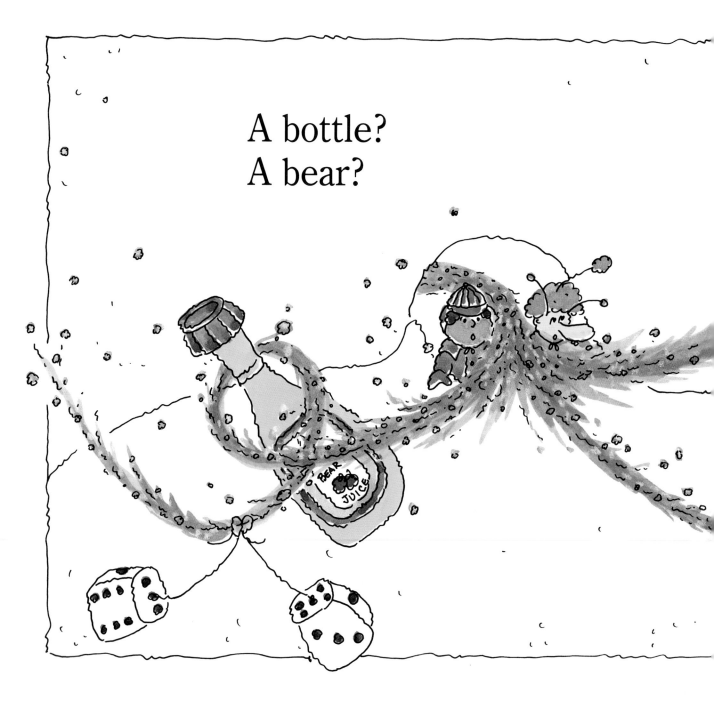

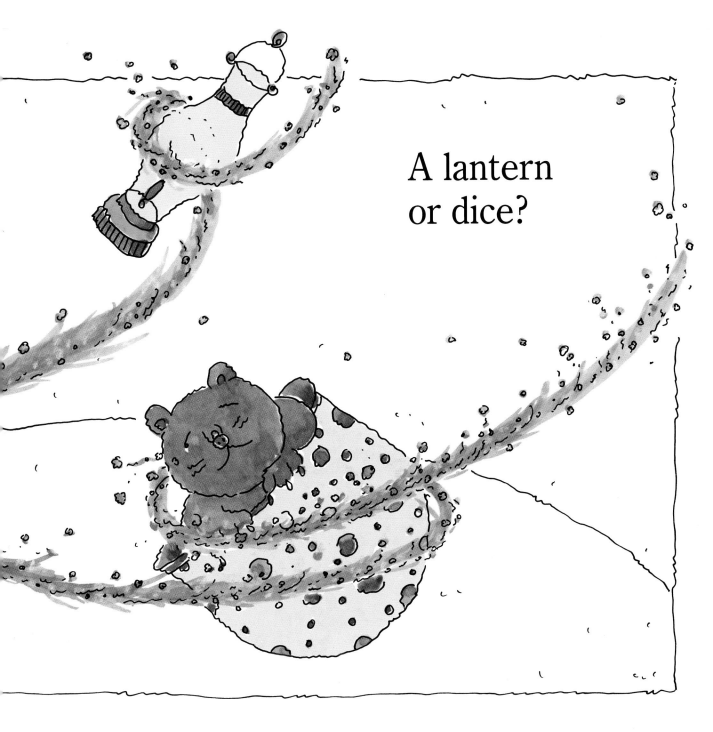

A lantern
or dice?

(A bear)

Food is scarce at this
time of the year.

It's hard for animals
when winter is here.